THE PUPPY PLACE

MOOSE

THE PUPPY PLACE

MOOSE

**ELLEN
MILES**

SCHOLASTIC INC.
New York   Toronto   London   Auckland
Sydney   Mexico City   New Delhi   Hong Kong

For Sarah and Tobey

No part of this publication may be reproduced, stored in a retrieval system, or transmitted in any form or by any means, electronic, mechanical, photocopying, recording, or otherwise, without written permission of the publisher. For information regarding permission, write to Scholastic Inc., Attention: Permissions Department, 557 Broadway, New York, NY 10012.

ISBN 978-0-545-25397-0

Cover art by Tim O'Brien
Original cover design by Steve Scott

12 11 10 9 8 7 6 5 4 3   11 12 13 14 15 16/0

Printed in the U.S.A.   40

First printing, March 2011

CHAPTER ONE

"Better ride fast!" Sammy pointed to the sky. "It's going to start raining any second."

"Don't worry, I'll make it." Charles Peterson waved at his best friend as he pushed off on his bike. Charles and Sammy usually biked to and from school together. But on this gloomy spring Thursday afternoon, Sammy's mom was picking him up to take him to a dentist appointment—so Charles had to ride home alone.

Charles glanced up as he rode past the playground. At recess that day, it had been sunny and warm. Now the sun had disappeared and the sky had turned gray. A strong wind began to blow, tossing the leaves in the trees. And right above him,

Charles saw dark clouds gathering together into a billowy black mountain that loomed overhead.

It was not a long ride home. Charles thought he could make it before the rain began, if he rode hard. He stood up on the pedals and began to rock his bike to and fro, using his arms as well as his legs to push harder, faster. The wind pushed back and made dark little whirlpools of road dust that sprayed grit into Charles's face. *Splat.* A fat, heavy raindrop smacked his helmet. *Splat. Splat. Splat.* Three more splashed his arms and face. Charles was already panting, but he ramped up his speed even more. Once, his dad had told him that if you went fast enough, you could dodge the raindrops and stay dry, even when it was pouring. Ha. Who could ever go *that* fast? Now Charles remembered the little smile on Dad's face when he'd said it, and realized it was just a joke.

The splats came faster and harder, and the road turned from gray to spotted to black as the rain poured down. Charles smelled that special rain-on-dusty-road smell rising from the pavement. He wiped away the drips running off his helmet's visor so he could see through the downpour. His sneakers were already squishing and cold rain trickled down the back of his neck.

What would Mysterioso do in this situation? Charles thought of the performer he'd seen at his school's Spring Fling fair. Round-bellied and short, with a shiny bald head, Mysterioso looked like an ordinary guy, maybe somebody's dad. But he was an amazing magician. Mysterioso could read minds, pull coins from your ear, and turn a red scarf into a yellow one, right in front of your eyes.

Charles had been thinking about that show a lot. Mysterioso had cracked jokes as he did his tricks, and the audience loved him. People were still talking about Mysterioso two weeks after the fair. Charles had already decided that he wanted to be a magician, too. He'd found a book on magic tricks at the library so he could learn to do what Mysterioso did.

Could Mysterioso make the rain stop pouring down? Charles looked up at the sky. "Abra-ca-doodle!" he shouted, remembering the magician's special word.

The rain did not stop. Charles had not really expected it to. Probably you also needed to wave a wand or sprinkle some magic powder or something.

Charles gave up and slowed down his pedaling. What was the point? He was so wet that he couldn't get any wetter. He was cold, too. He thought about how warm it would be at home, and how Mom would meet him at the door with a big fluffy towel so he could dry off. He would get out of these wet clothes as quickly as he could and change into his warm, dry sweatpants and his favorite Batman shirt. Maybe, if he was lucky,

Mom would make him a cup of cocoa and bring it to him on the couch, where he could cozy up with a blanket over him and Buddy at his feet.

Buddy was the Petersons' puppy. Charles loved him. He loved the way Buddy was always so happy to see him, wagging his tail so hard his whole body shook. He loved the way Buddy was always excited to find out what was next: Food? A car trip? Maybe some fun with a ball? Whatever it was, Buddy was up for it. And Charles loved the way Buddy slept next to him, curled up small with his chin propped on Charles's knee.

The Petersons had taken care of lots of puppies. They were a foster family, which meant they took in puppies who needed homes. Some puppies stayed a few days, others stayed a couple of weeks. But every single puppy went to the forever family that was just right for him or her. Buddy started out as a foster puppy. Then it turned out that Charles and his mom and dad, his older sister, Lizzie, and his younger brother, the Bean, were the perfect forever family for Buddy. So the little brown puppy with a heart-shaped white patch on his chest had come to stay.

Thinking about Buddy almost made Charles feel a little warmer, even though it did not make the rain stop. Charles sighed. He was only a few blocks from home, but it might as well have been miles.

Then he heard a rumble of thunder.

"Yikes," said Charles. He looked up at the sky. The tower of dark clouds had doubled in size. Now it looked like the giant's castle in "Jack and the Beanstalk," high above the earth.

Getting caught in the rain was one thing. Getting caught in a thunderstorm was another. Charles stood up on the pedals again and began to pump hard.

A car honked at him. Charles ignored it. He was biking way over on the side of the road, exactly where he should be. He concentrated on riding as fast as he could.

The car honked again. "Charles!" someone yelled.

Charles turned his head and saw his family's silver van rolling slowly along behind him. The passenger-side window was down and Mom was leaning over to call to him.

"Mom!" Charles was so glad to see her. He put on the brakes and got off his bike.

Mom pulled the van over and jumped out. "Oh, honey," she said. "You're soaked. Come on, let's get your bike in the back. I was on my way to take Lizzie to Aunt Amanda's place and I realized you must be riding home in this pouring rain."

Some days after school, Lizzie helped out at their aunt Amanda's doggy day-care center.

Bowser's Backyard could be a busy place some-times. People who worked all day and didn't want to leave their dogs alone brought them there, and sometimes Aunt Amanda had thirty dogs to care for. Her place was just like preschool for dogs, with nap time, snack time, and plenty of play-time. Because of the rain, Charles knew the dogs would be having indoor fun this afternoon in the big bright playroom filled with balls and other toys.

After they'd wrestled Charles's bike into the back of the van, Mom helped Charles get his wet T-shirt off and pull on the dry sweatshirt she'd brought for him. He kicked off his sneakers and put his feet under Buddy's ratty old car blanket. The smell of dog made him feel instantly better, and Mom cranked the heat as they took off to pick up Lizzie from school.

"You're late," Lizzie said as she climbed into the backseat. "Wow, what happened to you?" She stared at Charles. "You look like a drowned rat." Lizzie, who had waited inside the school's front doors, was dry as a bone.

"It's raining, for your information," Charles said. A roll of thunder grumbled overhead. "And there's a thunderstorm coming, too."

"I hope Buddy's not scared, at home all alone," Lizzie said.

"He's not alone," said Mom. "Dad and the Bean are there with him. Anyway, we're lucky. Buddy doesn't seem to be afraid of thunder." She pulled up in front of Aunt Amanda's. "I'll pick you up a little earlier than usual, at five-thirty," she told Lizzie. "Don't forget, you have to pack your things tonight."

Charles and Lizzie had a four-day weekend coming up. Charles didn't have any special plans, but Lizzie's class—in fact, the whole fourth grade—was going on a special trip to Boston. Lizzie had been talking about it for weeks.

Lizzie got out of the van and ran for the entrance of the doggy day care, yanking the door open just as a loud clap of thunder boomed overhead.

A streak of gray bolted past her, heading straight for the parking lot.

"Hey!" yelled Charles. "Is that a dog?"

CHAPTER TWO

Charles threw open the door of the van and leapt out, forgetting all about the rain, the thunderstorm, and his bare feet. "Oof!" He tackled the running dog, banging his knees and elbows on the pavement. "Hold on there," he said. "I've got you now." He hugged the dog close, noticing the way he shook and shivered with fear. "It's okay, big guy," he murmured into one of the dog's floppy ears.

The dog really *was* a big guy. He probably weighed more than Charles did. Charles had to lie on top of him, using all his weight to hold him still. There was another loud clap of thunder, and the dog tried to jump up.

Yeow! Get me out of here.

The dog squirmed desperately in Charles's arms. He was strong as well as big. But Charles hung on tightly and he did not get away.

"Moose!" Aunt Amanda stood at the door of her business. Her face was as white as chalk. "Oh, Moose. You nearly scared me to death." She rushed out to where Charles and the dog lay tangled in a heap on the ground. "Poor Moose," she said as she grabbed the dog's collar.

Poor Moose? Charles looked down at his wet jeans, now with holes torn in both knees. He rubbed his sore elbows. What about poor Charles?

"Great catch, Charles," Aunt Amanda called over her shoulder as she tugged Moose, tail between his legs, back toward the building. "I hate to think what might have happened if he'd made it out to the road."

Charles and Mom followed Aunt Amanda inside. "Poor dog. Was it the thunder that scared him?" Mom asked.

Aunt Amanda knelt on the floor and rubbed Moose down with a towel. She nodded. "This puppy is the biggest scaredy-cat I've ever seen."

"Puppy?" Charles asked. He'd never seen a puppy this big. His huge chunky head and giant chunky paws reminded Charles of Scooby-Doo's.

Aunt Amanda nodded. "He's not even a year old. He'll get even bigger than this when he fills out a little more." She let go of the puppy for a second and he shook himself off, shimmying his whole body from ears to tail.

Charles went over to pet Moose, hoping to help the scared puppy calm down. Moose pulled away at first, but Charles moved slowly, scratching Moose's ears until the big pup relaxed and leaned against him. Moose was a beautiful dog. His short, shiny coat was silvery gray, with black spots all over. He had a white bib on his chest and a white stripe up the middle of his face. Two of his big, chunky paws and the tip of his skinny tail were white, too. Moose was so tall that his head was on the same level as Charles's. His big brown eyes looked right back into Charles's, and Charles practically had to reach up to scratch his ears. It wasn't like petting Buddy, who came up to Charles's knees. "You're not a scaredy-cat," Charles said to Moose. "You're a scaredy-dog."

Lizzie and Mom laughed, but Aunt Amanda was still frowning. "It's not funny," she said. "Not really. I feel terrible for him. He's afraid of thunderstorms, he's afraid of mailboxes, he's afraid of little kids and wrapping paper. Oh, and the vacuum cleaner and the blender and anything that moves too fast or too suddenly. Moose is one petrified pup. He's afraid of his own shadow."

"Are all Great Danes like that?" asked Lizzie.

Charles was not surprised that Lizzie knew what breed the puppy was. She knew everything about dogs, and every night she studied the "Dog Breeds of the World" poster that hung on her bedroom wall.

But Aunt Amanda shook her head. "It's not a common behavior problem for the breed, as far as I know. It may be because Moose spent his first six months chained up behind someone's house. He wasn't exposed to much except the side of a garage, so everything is new and different to him." She sighed. "I really hate to have to tell the Brewers about this."

"The Brewers?" asked Mom.

"His owners. Al and Karine, and their little girl, Caroline. When his first owners decided they didn't want a dog after all, the Brewers adopted Moose and gave him a good home, and they all adore him. But this fear problem is getting to them. They can't take him anywhere, and they don't like to leave him home alone, either. He doesn't like to go to the dog park because he's afraid of other dogs—just the small ones, that is. And he totally freaks out whenever they take him to the vet. It's hard to control a big dog who's scared to death."

"Maybe he'll grow out of it," Lizzie said. She came over to stroke the puppy. Moose put his ears back and scooted closer to Charles.

"That's what the Brewers were hoping," said Aunt Amanda. "But so far it's only gotten worse. That's why they started bringing him to me. They thought that coming here might help him get used to being around other dogs, and they were hoping I could spend some time training him to be less fearful."

"How would you do that?" Charles asked. He knew how to teach a dog to sit or shake hands, but he couldn't imagine how you could teach a puppy not to be afraid of things.

"There are some ways, but it wouldn't be easy," Aunt Amanda said. "Helping a dog overcome his fears can take a lot of time. I'm worried that Moose's owners have already run out of patience with his problem."

It turned out that Aunt Amanda was right. Later that night, after dinner, she appeared at the Petersons'. "Is the Bean in bed?" she asked when Charles answered the door. Charles nodded. "Good," she said. "Maybe you'd better put Buddy in your room for a while, too." Then Charles saw Moose trying to hide behind Aunt Amanda, his big head down, his floppy ears back, and his tail tucked between his trembling legs.

CHAPTER THREE

Once they were all settled in the living room, Aunt Amanda explained. "Moose's owners were very upset when they heard about him trying to run away today. They said it was the last straw, and they asked me to find him another home."

"So we're going to foster him?" Lizzie asked eagerly. She had always wanted to foster a Great Dane. She loved big dogs.

Charles sat on the floor, with Moose lying next to him. The big puppy rested his head on Charles's knee. That was one heavy head. Charles's foot was already asleep. Charles stroked Moose's ears, scratching between them in the way he knew all dogs liked. "How can we?" he asked. "If he's afraid of little kids, the Bean would terrify him."

"That's right," said Aunt Amanda. "Anyway, it won't be necessary. I convinced the Brewers to give me one last chance at training Moose. I'm headed up to Camp Bowser this weekend with some other dogs, and they've agreed to let me take him along. If I can find a way to help Moose start to overcome his fears, they'll consider keeping him."

Camp Bowser was Aunt Amanda and Uncle James's place in the country. They went up there often with their own dogs, and sometimes took a few of their clients' dogs along as well. Charles had heard all about Camp Bowser: he knew about the cute little cabin with the screened-in Pooch Porch for dogs to nap on, the creek for them to play in, the wonderful home-baked doggy treats Aunt Amanda made. Lizzie had been up there twice, but so far, Charles had never gotten to go.

"I'll need some help, though," said Aunt Amanda. "That's why I'm here. Since I'll have other dogs to watch, I think Moose needs a companion for the weekend, someone who can be with him every minute."

"I'd love to," said Lizzie, as if Aunt Amanda had invited her.

Mom held up a hand. "Lizzie," she said. "What about your trip to Boston?"

Lizzie's face fell. "Oh," she said. "Well, maybe I could—"

"Actually," said Aunt Amanda, "I was going to ask Charles this time." She smiled at him. "It seems as if you and Moose have already become friends. I think he trusts you, Charles."

Charles felt his face grow hot, and knew he was

blushing. It was very flattering that a frightened dog like Moose would feel safe with him. And it was an even bigger compliment for Aunt Amanda to want him along on this special weekend. "Wow," he said. "Can I, Mom? Can I go?"

Mom looked at Dad. He nodded, and they both smiled. "Sure," she said, turning back to Charles. "I think Moose needs you. I guess that means you and Lizzie *both* have some packing to do tonight."

"I'm just wondering," Dad asked Aunt Amanda, "why would a dog become so fearful to begin with?"

"It's hard to say," said Aunt Amanda. "Some dogs have a bad experience as puppies, and it sticks with them. For example, one dog I knew was kicked by a big man when she was a little puppy, so she was afraid of large men from then on. Other scaredy-dogs were never socialized enough. That may be the case with Moose. After the Brewers adopted him, they spent a lot of time at their country house, so he didn't meet many other dogs or people. They finally started to take him to obedience classes, and that's been great for him. But since he didn't have a variety of experiences when he was younger, every new thing scares him."

"So how can you teach him not to be scared?" asked Lizzie.

"Dog trainers have lots of different methods," said Aunt Amanda. "I think the best way is probably desensitization."

"De-*what*?" asked Charles.

"I know, it's a big word," said Aunt Amanda. "Basically, it just means helping the dog become less sensitive to scary things by introducing them slowly and carefully, a little bit at a time."

Charles was interested. "Like how?"

"Okay," said Aunt Amanda. "Let's say Moose

is afraid of . . ." She looked around the room. "Squeaky toys," she said, spotting Buddy's favorite toy, Mr. Duck. "Which he is, probably because they make a sudden noise that surprises him."

She went over and picked up Mr. Duck. "Some trainers believe in a technique called 'flooding,'" she said. "They think that you should expose the dog to whatever scares him until he just gets used to it. They would take Mr. Duck right up close to Moose and make the toy squeak over and over."

"That's mean." Charles put his arm around Moose. Moose sighed and settled in closer to Charles, leaning his full, heavy weight against him. "I would never do that to a dog."

"Neither would I," said Aunt Amanda. "What I would do is first try to get Moose used to having Mr. Duck around. I would leave Mr. Duck where Moose could see him, and if Moose happened to go over on his own to check out the toy I would praise him and give him treats, so he would be rewarded for being curious and brave."

"And then?" asked Lizzie. "What about the squeaky part?"

"Noises can be very scary for dogs," said Aunt Amanda. "Remember, their hearing is even better than ours, so even a small noise can sound loud. I would start by taking Mr. Duck far away before I made him squeak." She carried Mr. Duck over to the fireplace and gave him a tiny squeeze.

A small squeak came out, and Moose's ears perked but he did not get up to run away. "Good boy." Charles stroked the big dog's cheek. It was like petting a horse's jaw.

"That's exactly right, Charles. Reward him for being brave," said Aunt Amanda. "Then, over time, I would slowly bring Mr. Duck closer and closer, making him squeak and giving Moose pats and treats if he did not run away. I might also try to distract Moose with some other activity, like having him do a trick for me. Finally, hopefully, Moose would be able to have Mr. Duck squeak right there next to him."

"Wow," said Lizzie. "That's a lot of work."

Aunt Amanda nodded. "It sure is. And it takes a lot of time. But if we can get him started, I think the Brewers would be happy to keep working with him. They've really enjoyed getting into obedience training with Moose, and they really do love him."

"Who wouldn't love this guy?" Charles gave Moose a kiss on the nose. Moose kissed him back, licking his cheek with a giant, slurpy tongue.

You're my pal, aren't you?

"Well," said Aunt Amanda, "Moose and I had better get going. Can you be ready first thing tomorrow morning, Charles? We want to leave early."

"I'll be ready," Charles promised. He couldn't wait to be at Camp Bowser with Moose.

CHAPTER FOUR

Packing for his weekend away was easy. Getting up early? A breeze. The only hard part about going to Camp Bowser, thought Charles, was saying good-bye to Buddy. Now, sitting in the backseat of Aunt Amanda's van, Charles remembered how Buddy had looked up at him so hopefully when he put his duffel bag by the door. "Sorry, Buddy," Charles had told him as he sat down to give him a hug. "You're not coming with me this time. I wish you could, but I think you might scare Moose. You stay home and keep Mom and Dad and the Bean company, okay?" Charles was not sure that Buddy understood, but he had given him lots of extra-special hugs and pats while he waited for Aunt Amanda to pick him up.

"Buddy's going to miss you and Lizzie this weekend," said Aunt Amanda now, catching Charles's eye in the rearview mirror. It was as if she had read his mind. "Your parents will, too. The house will be awfully quiet with both of you away."

Charles nodded. At the moment, he had a lump in his throat that made it hard to answer. He hoped he would not feel too homesick up at Camp Bowser. He looked over at Moose, who was snoozing in an enormous crate next to Charles's seat. A few other crates were crammed into the back of the van, holding more dogs who were on their way north for a weekend of fun in the country. Aunt Amanda had brought her dog, Bowser (the golden retriever her business was named after), but she had left her three pugs home with Uncle James so the little dogs wouldn't scare Moose.

"We're going to have a good time, Moose," Charles said softly. "I bet you'll love it at Camp Bowser."

Moose opened his eyes and looked up at Charles, worried wrinkles furrowing his big forehead.

Really? Are you sure? Because I think it might be kind of scary.

Charles poked a finger through the crate to scratch Moose's ear. "It'll be fine. You'll see." Moose sighed and went back to sleep, head on crossed paws.

"I'm counting on you to keep a close eye on Moose this whole weekend and be his pal," said Aunt Amanda. "If there's another thunderstorm, or something else frightens him, the best thing to do is distract him so he doesn't focus on the scary thing. Talk gently to him, but don't baby him. Give him some treats so he has a happy experience instead of a frightening one. Can you do that?"

"Sure," said Charles. He patted his pocket, where there were four or five small dog biscuits. He always carried treats, just in case he met a dog he wanted to make friends with.

Then he reached into his backpack and pulled out the deck of cards he'd brought along. He had also packed *1-2-3 Magic*, the book he hoped to learn some tricks from. He planned to start with card tricks, since those seemed the simplest. There was only one problem. Even though *1-2-3 Magic* was supposedly for beginners, the author started the directions for every card trick with "Shuffle the cards. . . ."

Charles did not know how to shuffle. When he and Sammy played war, which they some-times did for hours at a time on rainy days, Sammy always shuffled. Charles suspected that Sammy sometimes shuffled some of the better cards into his half of the deck. It might be good if he learned to shuffle, too.

He opened the little box of cards and shook them out. "Oops!" They slid out of his hands and spilled all over the floor of the van.

"What do you have there, Charles?" Aunt Amanda looked at him in the mirror again.

"Just some cards." Charles scooped up as many as he could reach. He wasn't ready to tell anyone that he was learning magic. He wanted to surprise everyone once he had some great tricks ready. He split the deck into two parts and tried shoving them together, but most of them fell into his lap. He scooped them up again and tried shuffling another way, the way Sammy did it where he flipped the corners together. That was even worse. The ace of spades, the queen of hearts, and the four of diamonds ended up inside Moose's crate. Moose was so fast asleep that he did not even twitch.

Charles kept picking up the cards and

practicing. But by the time Aunt Amanda turned off the main highway and drove up a long, bumpy dirt road, he had still not learned to shuffle. When the van came to a stop, he shoved the cards into his backpack and zipped it shut. "Is this it?" he asked. "Is this Camp Bowser?"

"That's right," said Aunt Amanda. "Welcome."

In the middle of a clearing in the woods, a tiny cabin peeked out from behind two tall pine trees, reminding Charles of the way Moose had peeked out from behind Aunt Amanda at the Petersons' front door the night before.

Birdsong drifted out from the woods, and a sweet, piney smell filled the air. Charles took a long, deep breath and smiled. Camp Bowser was all right.

"I like to take all the dogs down to play in the stream first thing when we get here," said Aunt Amanda as she opened up the back of the van, "so they can stretch their legs." She unlatched Moose's crate and led him out on his leash. Charles unbuckled his seat belt and got out, too.

Moose yawned and shook himself, setting his floppy ears flapping. Then he lay down and began to roll in the grass, happily stretching his legs this way and that as he squirmed and scratched his whole long back on the ground.

This feels so good, it makes me forget about being scared!

Then he jumped up, with a jingle of collar tags, and began to sniff all around.

I smell other dogs here. I hope they're not those little ones who like to nip at my ankles.

Aunt Amanda stood holding the leash, smiling at Moose. "This is how he gets to know a new place," she said to Charles. "It's only fair to let him sniff a little." After he had rolled and sniffed for a while longer, she said, "Moose, come." Moose whirled around at the end of the leash and came right over to sit as still as a statue, in front of and facing Aunt Amanda, with his ears perked up and his eyes focused on her eyes. "Good boy," she said.

"Wow," said Charles. "He sure does listen to you."

"Bowser wasn't this well trained until he was at least three years old," Aunt Amanda told Charles. "All the obedience training the Brewers have done has really paid off." She looked down at Moose and made a hand signal, tapping her left thigh. "Heel, Moose," she said.

Moose practically leapt into the air in his eagerness to obey, landing in another perfect sit at Aunt Amanda's side. "Let's go," she said to Moose as she took a step forward. Moose stuck to her side like glue, looking up at her face to watch for any clues about which way they were going.

Charles was impressed. Buddy was a good dog, and he could sit and shake hands and stuff like that, but Moose was amazing. Aunt Amanda handed Moose's leash over to Charles and began to get the other dogs out of the van.

At first, Charles was a little nervous. Moose was almost taller than he was, and he looked like he could pull somebody over in a second. Charles cleared his throat. "Um . . . heel, Moose," he said. And Moose heeled! He stuck right to Charles's left side as Charles practiced walking the big puppy up and down. He didn't even have to give the commands; Moose walked calmly next to him without one bit of pulling or jumping or lagging behind, all the things Buddy usually did on a leash.

They all walked down to the stream together. Bowser led the way through the tall grass, his feathery tail waving proudly as he showed off his place to the other dogs. He didn't have to be on a leash, but Aunt Amanda had clipped leashes onto the dogs she'd brought: Tobey, a young chocolate Lab, and Sofie, a basset mix. They romped after Bowser, sniffing at everything. Closer to the stream, the path through the grass became a trail through the woods, with rocks and roots underfoot and bright green ferns and mosses lining the sides. All the way down the trail, Moose walked very nicely next to Charles, without any tugging.

Soon they came to a little pool by a waterfall. The dogs splashed around in the cool, clear water, chasing frogs and wetting their bellies and sticking their snouts in for long, slurpy drinks. Even Moose waded in up to his ankles, though he jumped right back out when a tadpole tickled his snout. Then Aunt Amanda said it was time to head back and finish unpacking the van.

Charles led the way back up the path, with

Moose still walking like a perfect gentleman right at his side. Then something slithered across the rocky trail. A little snake! Just a tiny one, a garter snake that Charles knew would never hurt anybody. Charles saw it first and tightened his grip on Moose's leash. Then Moose spotted it and stopped short.

Yikes!

The big dog leapt sideways into the air, then took off at a mad gallop, pulling Charles right over and dragging him along.

CHAPTER FIVE

"Whooaaa!" Charles hung on tightly as Moose charged down the path. "Ouch! Ow! Ooh!" Charles did not let go of the leash, even when rocks scraped his belly and roots banged his elbows.

"Moose!" yelled Aunt Amanda. "Down!"

Instantly, Moose stopped in his tracks and lay down.

"Wow," Charles said from where he lay behind Moose. "He really is obedient, isn't he?"

"Stay," Aunt Amanda said to Moose. "Stay right there." Moose gazed up at her and did not move a muscle. Aunt Amanda ran over to help Charles up. "Are you okay?" she asked. "I am so sorry about that. I guess we have to remember that anything unfamiliar is scary to Moose."

"I'm fine." Charles dusted off his knees and rubbed his sore elbows. "That was cool, how fast he lay down when you told him to."

"That was terrific," Aunt Amanda agreed. "I wasn't positive he would obey but I thought it was worth a try. It's great to have a dog who will do that. I call it an 'emergency down.' It could save his life someday, like if he were about to run out into a busy street."

For the rest of the day, Charles stuck to Moose like glue. He did his best to make sure that nothing scared the huge puppy, but it wasn't easy. Moose panicked when Aunt Amanda brought out the Frisbee to play catch with the other dogs. He leapt high into the air when a cricket jumped out of the grass near his chin. At nap time, he circled endlessly on the Pooch Porch before he could find a sleeping spot that felt right to him. And when Tobey found a squeaky toy and started chewing it, Moose nearly hit the ceiling.

By the end of the afternoon, Charles was tired—and frustrated. Moose was such a great dog—but who would have the patience to deal with him if he kept freaking out all the time? It would not be easy to find a forever family for him.

For dinner, Aunt Amanda made mac and cheese out of a box. "Sorry," she told Charles as they sat down at the kitchen table to eat. "We always end up eating this the first night up here. I'll make something better tomorrow."

"Are you kidding?" Charles took a big forkful. "I love this stuff."

"That's right." Aunt Amanda dug into her own serving. "There was a while when you were the Bean's age when you wouldn't eat anything else."

Charles didn't remember that, but his mother always said it, too, so it must be true. He looked down at Moose, who lay snoozing near his feet. "Camp Bowser is even more fun than I imagined," he told Aunt Amanda. "I think Moose is having a really good time—at least, when he's not petrified."

"I agree," said Aunt Amanda. "But he needs to learn something, too. That's why he came along with us this weekend, after all. I'm just still not sure of the best way to help him."

If Aunt Amanda didn't know, who did? Charles noticed a wooden holder in the middle of the table, stacked with little red, white, and blue plastic discs. "What are those?" he asked, pointing with his fork.

"Poker chips," said his aunt. "Uncle James and I have some friends up here who like to come over for a friendly game now and then."

"You play poker?" Charles asked. He was surprised. He had never pictured his aunt as a poker player. Hmm . . . Maybe she could help him. "So, do you know how to shuffle cards?"

"Sure." Aunt Amanda nodded. "I'd be happy to teach you. Ready for seconds?" She pushed back her chair to go to the stove. The scraping sound woke Moose, who jumped up and began to pace around, whining and panting.

What was that? What was that noise?

"Oh, Moose," said Aunt Amanda. "It's okay. Take it easy, boy."

Charles patted the floor near his chair. "Down, Moose," he said. Moose came right over and lay down. "Why is he panting?" Charles asked. "It's not hot in here."

"Sometimes dogs pant when they're stressed

out," Aunt Amanda told him. "He'll settle down soon. I still don't know how we're going to help Moose, but I'm sure glad you came along. I can tell that having you nearby all the time helps him feel more secure."

Charles blushed and ducked his head. He petted Moose some more. Hearing that from Aunt Amanda made him feel good. Maybe he really could help Moose.

After dinner, Charles helped tidy up the kitchen. Then he and his aunt went into the living room and sat on the faded blue rag rug, with the low coffee table between them. Bowser claimed the best spot on the couch, and the other dogs settled in, too. Moose curled up right next to Charles, leaning his big head on Charles's knee. Soon all of the dogs were snoring in different tones as Aunt Amanda showed Charles how to shuffle cards. It was cozy in the little cabin.

After the lesson, they played war for a long time while the dogs slept peacefully around them. Charles did all the shuffling, just for practice.

By the time he and Moose went to bed, Charles was so sleepy he could hardly keep his eyes open. But after he'd changed into his pajamas, he pulled out *Magic 1-2-3* and read through the directions for a card trick called Count-'Em-Out. Now that he knew how to shuffle, the rest would be easy.

CHAPTER SIX

"It's okay, Moose," Charles said sleepily. He opened one eye and saw that it was still dark in his bedroom. "Go back to sleep." He reached out to touch the big puppy, who was pacing up and down next to Charles's bed, his collar tags jingling as he walked. "What's the matter, anyway?"

Moose whimpered and licked Charles's hand.

I hear something. Something that scares me.

Charles sat up and patted the bed, wiping the slobber off his hand at the same time. "Come on up here with me," he told Moose. "Come on, boy. What's so scary?" Moose jumped up and lay down, taking over most of the bed and squishing Charles up against the wall. Now that it was quiet in the room again, Charles could hear what was worrying Moose: *pit-pat, pit-a-pat*, the sound of rain on the roof. "That's just rain," he told Moose. "That doesn't mean there will be thunder, too." He petted the puppy's big head until Moose gave a long sigh and settled down to sleep.

"The rain on the roof last night scared Moose," Charles reported when he and the big pup went downstairs to eat breakfast in the morning. It had cleared up by then, and bright sunshine poured through the windows as Aunt Amanda bustled around, frying bacon and putting out food for the dogs. She set Moose's dish way off to the side so he could eat without worrying about the other dogs.

Aunt Amanda shook her head. "Oh, dear. And the weatherman said there'll be more rain—and maybe another storm—later on today." She put a plate full of scrambled eggs and bacon down in front of Charles. "Here's what I think," she said. "You and Moose should get some outdoor exercise now, while it's sunny. Then you should just spend a quiet day together, staying off to yourselves so that Moose isn't stressed and fearful. He can't learn anything when he's in that state."

"Sounds good to me," said Charles around a mouthful of eggs. "How about you, Moose?" Moose ambled over to lick Charles's face.

Yum! I love eggs and bacon.

Charles laughed. "Who needs a napkin when you have a Great Dane?" he asked. He was almost getting used to how huge Moose was.

When he'd finished breakfast, Charles called Moose and clipped a leash onto the big dog's collar.

"I doubt he'll pull you over again," said Aunt Amanda. "But if he does take off, just remember this: let go of the leash—and yell 'down.' That should stop him in his tracks, and you won't get dragged along the trail."

Charles nodded. He wished he'd known about that trick the day before. "Got it," he said. "Ready, Moose? Let's go to the stream."

The enormous puppy walked nicely, prancing along at Charles's side as they set off toward the stream. The long grass was still wet from the night's rain, and droplets glistened like diamonds on the new green leaves that covered the trees. It was a beautiful morning, and the air was full of delicious, fresh smells. Charles and Moose both sniffed happily as they walked.

Charles loved to watch Moose move. He had an elegant gait, like a fancy horse that lifts its hooves daintily with every step. Moose seemed a little more confident this morning, too. His head was up and his ears were perked, listening to the birdsong that surrounded them as they moved through the meadow.

But as they entered the woods and the trail became rocky, Charles noticed that Moose began to walk more cautiously, looking around as he placed one chunky foot after the other. He stuck right to Charles's side. Suddenly, the big dog stopped in his tracks.

Here! It was here. That slithery, slinky thing was right here.

"Come on, Moose." Charles tugged on the leash. But when Moose didn't want to move, there was no way Charles was strong enough to make him. Moose put his ears back and stared wide-eyed at the ground around his feet. "Oh," said Charles. "I get it. This is where you saw the snake." Charles wasn't sure what to do, but he did not want to force poor Moose to do something that was scary.

"Okay," he said, sighing. "Forget the stream. Let's go back to the cabin." Moose seemed to like that idea. But halfway through the meadow, he suddenly leapt into the air and came down wild-eyed and snorting. "It's okay, boy." Charles stopped and sighed again. "It's just another cricket." He led Moose down another trail, hoping that this time they wouldn't run into anything scary. But Moose was frightened by everything: a bird that flew too close, the neon-green Frisbee that had been left in the grass, and a chipmunk that hopped onto the mossy stone wall and chittered at the big dog.

Charles kept leading Moose down one trail after another, hoping to at least tire the puppy out. They had gone farther from the cabin than he'd meant to go, but Charles was sure he knew the way back. The sun felt blazingly hot out in the meadow, so Charles strayed deep into some piney woods in search of shade. But by the time he and Moose came back out of the woods, the sun was gone and the sky was gray. Charles shivered. It wasn't so hot anymore now that the sun had disappeared. He tugged on Moose's leash. "Come on, boy, let's head back."

They'd only gone a few steps before the wind began to blow.

A mountain of dark clouds began to gather overhead.

And a big, fat raindrop smacked Charles's cheek.

CHAPTER SEVEN

"Uh-oh," Charles said to himself. He glanced up at the sky again and saw that the mountain of clouds overhead was just as big and just as black as the one he'd seen on the day he first met Moose. He knew what that meant. A thunderstorm. What would happen if Moose panicked while they were out here in the open?

"Okay, Moose." Charles tugged on the leash and began to walk. "We have to get moving. We have to get back to the cabin."

But Moose already knew something was up. His ears went back and Charles could see the whites of the big pup's eyes as he stared straight ahead.

Moose sat down, dug in his front paws, and began to pant.

I'm not going anywhere. I'm too scared. I'm staying right here.

Charles tugged on the leash. He tugged harder. He leaned back and pulled as hard as he could, putting all his weight into it as if he were in a tug-of-war contest. But that big puppy Moose was like a statue. Charles could not make him budge.

Another raindrop hit Charles's head, then another and another. This was terrible. They had to get back to the cabin before the storm broke loose. Charles tried to think. What would Aunt Amanda do? He pictured her the day before, when she had first let Moose out of the van. After she'd let him sniff for a while and roll in the grass, she had given him some commands. Moose had obeyed instantly. He had obeyed when she told him "down" after he saw the snake, too. Moose always obeyed right away—if you knew what to say.

And suddenly, Charles *did* know what to say. He remembered exactly how Aunt Amanda had told Moose what she wanted from him. Would it work again? It was certainly worth a try. Charles stood up straight and spoke in his firmest voice. "Come, Moose."

Moose stood up and pranced right over to land in a perfect sit, facing Charles. "Wow. Good boy," Charles said. For a second, he couldn't believe it had worked—but it really had. Still, it was only a start. Next, he slapped his left thigh. "Heel, Moose," he said.

Moose jumped up and spun around, landing in another perfect sit close to Charles's left side. It was amazing how quick and precise he was for such a big dog. Charles smiled. "Good boy, Moose. Let's go." He took a step forward, just as he remembered Aunt Amanda doing, and Moose stepped forward at the exact same instant, sticking to Charles's side like glue. He looked up at Charles as he stepped along.

Is this what you wanted?

"Oh, you're such a good boy," said Charles. It was like magic, the way Moose forgot all his fears when he had a job to do. Charles walked quickly with Moose at his side, making his way back up the trail toward the cabin. Back through the piney woods they went. Back toward the meadow and the stone wall and the little cozy cabin. Raindrops were falling faster now, and Charles was nearly as soaked as he had been two days before on his bike. Moose hardly seemed to notice the rain, now that he was concentrating on following Charles's commands.

Then Charles heard a rumble of thunder.

He just barely heard it. It was way far off in the distance. Just a little drumroll to announce the coming storm.

Moose heard it, too. He was still looking up at Charles, but now his ears were back and the whites of his eyes showed again.

What was that?

"Let's go, Moose," Charles said firmly, slapping his thigh again. "Heel." Moose kept walking as Charles picked up the pace, but Charles could tell that his attention was not what it had been. The big dog's head kept whipping around as if he thought someone was sneaking up behind him.

The magic wasn't working anymore. Charles had to think of a new trick. "Moose, Moose, Moose," he said out loud, hoping to drown out the sound of any more thunder. Then he thought of the way that everyone in his family liked to sing silly songs to Buddy. They each had their own special song. Mom sang, *"Buddy Buddy Bo-Buddy, banana-fana fo-fuddy, me-mi-mo-muddy, Buddy!"* It was an old song called "The Name Game." Dad sang another old song called "Wooly Bully" as he tossed Buddy his stuffed sheep. Lizzie crooned sappy songs like "Buddy the Wonder Dog," and the Bean liked to sing *"Buddy, Buddy, little dog, How I wonder what you are,"* to the tune of "Twinkle, Twinkle, Little Star." Charles usually sang silly made-up words to whatever tune was in his head, usually stuff about how perfect and cute Buddy was.

"Moose, Moose, you silly goose!" Charles began to sing at the top of his lungs as he marched along, slapping his thigh. *"Heel by me, you big old Moose!"*

It worked. Moose looked, a little confused, but he moved along at a good clip, prancing at Charles's side. He even kept up when Charles, hearing another low rumble, began to run and sing at the same time. *"Moose, Moose, get in the caboose!"* Charles bellowed. *"Don't you let those cows get loose!"*

They reached the cabin just as the skies opened up and it really started to pour. A clap of thunder sounded overhead as Charles slammed the screen door shut behind them, and a terrified Moose tried to leap into Aunt Amanda's arms.

"Thank goodness you're back," she said. She petted Moose and whispered soothing words until he settled down and began to pace around the kitchen, panting. Another loud clap of thunder made the windows rattle in their frames. Moose scrambled under the table.

"Follow me," said Aunt Amanda. "Come, Moose." She led Charles and Moose down the hall to a small room Charles hadn't seen before. "This is where I do yoga in the mornings sometimes," she said. "It's the quietest room in the cabin, once you close the door. Plus, there are no windows for Moose to jump out of, or outside doors to escape through. Stay in here with Moose, and I'll bring you some dry clothes."

Charles nodded. "Okay," he croaked. His throat was sore from all the singing, but that didn't matter. What mattered was Moose. How would Charles keep him calm while the storm still raged outside?

CHAPTER EIGHT

There wasn't much in the yoga room, just a futon couch, a thick red rug, and a low table holding a CD player and a stack of CDs. Moose paced up and down, panting and whining quietly. Even with the door closed, Charles could still hear thunder rumbling. He knew Moose could, too.

"I'd sing some more for you," he rasped to Moose, "but my throat's too sore." Charles rummaged through the pile of CDs and found one by the Beatles. Soon, happy, upbeat music filled the room, covering any other sounds from outside.

"That's better, isn't it?" Charles asked Moose. They sat on the couch together, Charles with his legs crossed, and Moose with his front legs on the floor and his haunches up on the couch. Charles had to reach way up to scratch Moose's big head.

By the time Aunt Amanda came in to bring Charles a towel and some dry clothes, Moose was actually napping, even though the music still blasted. "Good work. I'm glad he's calmer," she said. "The storm is nearly over now. It's moving farther away every minute."

"I think we'll stay in here a while anyway," said Charles. "Can you bring me a deck of cards?" He might as well practice his trick while he sat out the storm with Moose.

Charles changed his clothes while he waited. It felt great to be dry again. Moose's short fur was already dry, too, after the rubdown Charles had given him with the towel.

When Aunt Amanda came back with the cards, Charles shook them out of their box and shuffled.

Moose woke up and stared wild-eyed at the cards.

"Oh, did that scare you?" Charles asked. "They're just cards, see?" Gently, he held out the cards so Moose could sniff them. He riffled their edges to make a little sound. Then he shuffled again, trying to do it more quietly. Moose jumped up and began to pace around.

"Sit, Moose," said Charles. Moose sat, right in front of the couch where Charles was sitting. He stared at Charles, waiting for another command. "Sit, stay, and watch," said Charles. He shuffled again. Moose's ears went back, but he stayed put. "Good boy," said Charles. "Down."

Moose lay down, his eyes darting between Charles's face and his hands. Charles shuffled again, and this time Moose didn't flinch. Having a job to do—even if it was only lying down and staying put—seemed to help. It made Moose concentrate on something besides whatever it was that was scaring him. It had worked outside in the rain, and it was working again now.

"Good boy," said Charles. He put Moose through a few more "sits" and "downs" while he shuffled, until Moose didn't seem to mind the cards at all. In fact, he seemed fascinated by them, and watched every move that Charles made.

Charles began to practice the Count-'Em-Out trick from his book. First you had to know which card was on top of the deck; then you had to *pretend* to shuffle while keeping that card on top. The whole trick depended on that. Charles put the two of diamonds on top, then tried to shuffle so that it stayed there.

Moose watched closely as Charles shuffled the cards, over and over again. They were both so focused on the cards that Charles was surprised when the Beatles CD ended. He realized that it was quiet outside. The storm had passed. He got up to put some more music on anyway, since he wanted to keep practicing his trick.

He flipped through the CDs—and then stopped, staring at one of them. *Sounds of Nature*, it was called, and it had a dramatic picture of a lightning strike on the cover. He flipped it over and looked at the contents. "'Rushing Stream,' 'Loons Calling at Dusk,' 'Crashing Surf,'—hey, look. 'Summer Thunderstorm,'" he read out loud to Moose.

Moose ambled over to see what Charles was talking about.

"Maybe we can use this to de-sensify, de-whatever-it-was you to the sound of thunder," said Charles. Moose cocked his head and stared at him.

Huh?

"See," Charles explained, "if I put this CD on with the volume way down, you'll hear the thunder—but just barely. We can do some obedience things like sit and come and down and stay to keep you distracted while it's playing. I'll give you some treats, too. And a lot of petting. Then, little by little, I can turn up the volume—just like I shuffled the cards quietly at first and then more loudly. After a while, maybe you won't mind the sound of thunder anymore."

Moose cocked his head the other way. Charles knew there was no way the big pup could actually understand what he was saying. But now Charles was excited. He really thought he might be onto something. Maybe this was the way to help Moose overcome his fears.

Charles and Moose spent the rest of that afternoon in the yoga room. They worked for a while on getting Moose used to the thunder sounds on the CD. Then Charles practiced his card trick some more, with Moose watching every move. Then they worked on the thunder sounds again. By the time Aunt Amanda poked her head in to say that dinner was almost ready, Charles thought he and Moose were almost ready, too: ready to show off everything they had learned.

CHAPTER NINE

"Ready?" As soon as they'd finished dinner and cleared away the dishes and made sure all the dogs were fed and walked and comfortable, Charles held up the deck of cards and waved it at his aunt. His heart thumped and his hands were sweaty. Doing a trick in front of another person was a lot harder than doing it alone, or in front of a dog. "Okay, here's my card trick. I want you to take this deck and deal out eight cards, just like this." Charles dealt out eight cards, counting out loud, "One, two, three, four, five, six, seven, eight." Then he picked up the little pile, put it on top of the rest of the deck, and handed it over to Aunt Amanda. "Now you do it."

Moose watched closely as the deck changed hands.

Aunt Amanda paused. "Why eight cards?" Amanda asked.

"Um, because eight is my lucky number?" Charles said. He had already started to worry that the trick was not going to go right. Now he remembered that the bit about his lucky number should have been part of his patter. "Patter" was all the things a magician said while he was working with the cards, and it was a big part of magic. If you talked quickly and made funny jokes, it took people's minds off what your hands were doing. Mysterioso had excellent patter.

"Okay," said Aunt Amanda. She got ready to count out the cards, but then she stopped. "So, can I shuffle these?"

Charles gulped. He'd been so nervous, and in so much of a rush, that he had totally forgotten the very first step. *He* was supposed to shuffle the cards, in front of his audience, so that they would think the cards were all shuffled—even though he knew that the two of diamonds was on top, because he had put it there. He had practiced all day. How could he have forgotten?

Moose stepped forward and nuzzled Charles's ear.

Everything okay? You seem upset.

Charles smiled at Moose. The big dog seemed to sense that something was wrong. "It's okay, Moose. No big deal." He turned to Aunt Amanda. "Sure, go ahead and shuffle," he said, even though he knew he had totally messed up the trick.

If he were a real magician like Mysterioso, he would have some other trick he could do now, to cover his mistake. But he had only learned one trick so far, and as Charles watched Aunt Amanda shuffle the cards, he knew he had botched it.

Sure, he could try to set up another card on top of the deck, but it would be hard without her noticing. He would just have to practice a whole lot more until he got this trick right.

"So, now I count out the cards?" Aunt Amanda asked when she was done shuffling.

"Know what?" Charles asked. "Never mind. I want to show you what Moose has learned. That's better than any magic trick."

Aunt Amanda smiled and put the cards down. "Great," she said. "I can't wait."

Charles began by telling Moose to sit, then lie down.

Aunt Amanda raised an eyebrow, as if she were wondering what the big deal was.

"That's not the good part," Charles said. "Watch this. Stay," he told the big dog. Charles had brought the CD player into the living room. Now, while Moose lay perfectly still with his huge paws crossed in front of him, Charles went over and pushed "play," so that the thunderstorm noises would begin.

Very softly, a rumbling sound filled the room. Charles went back to Moose and had him stand up, then sit again, then heel for a while around the room. He doled out treats from his pocket, along with lots of petting and lots of praise. Moose was doing great. He barely seemed to notice the rumblings and booms of recorded thunder. Each time Charles passed the CD player, he turned it up just a notch. Now Aunt Amanda nodded and smiled as she watched.

Charles took Moose on one more lap around the room, then told him to sit and stay. Moose sat very still, his head tilted and his ears perked, waiting for the next command. Charles walked over to turn up the CD player a tiny bit more, then turned and called, "Come, Moose."

Moose came charging over in his usual way. But instead of landing in a perfect sit in front of Charles, he skidded across the bare wood floor. Charles stepped backward to get out of the way and collided with a coatrack, knocking it over with a loud clatter. Moose leapt high into the air.

Yikes-a-rooni! Save me!

The big puppy dashed behind the couch and crouched there, trembling and whining.

Charles groaned. They'd been doing so well. He went over to turn off the CD player—and turned *up* the volume by mistake. *Bang! Crash!* Rolls of thunder and the flash of lightning filled the room. Charles fumbled with the buttons and finally managed to turn the CD off, but by then Moose was trying to get *under* the couch. "Sorry, sorry, sorry, Moose," said Charles, running over to pet him. "It's okay. The storm is over. You're okay."

Moose trembled and shook.

I'm not so sure about that. The noise is coming to get me!

Aunt Amanda knelt down by Moose, too. "He'll be fine," she told Charles.

"But now he's worse than ever. I ruined everything. All that work we did is wasted." Charles was so frustrated he almost felt like crying.

Aunt Amanda put her arms around Charles. "No, it's not," she said. "It's just like your magic trick. It takes a long time and a lot of practice to get a trick right. And it will take a long time and a lot of work to help Moose get over his fears. But you've made a great start. I can see that. And the Brewers would be able to use your method with all his other fears, too."

"Moose really is a great dog," Charles said,

sniffing. "If the Brewers decide not to keep him, I'm going to ask Mom and Dad if we can. I've only known him a few days, but he's already my pal." Charles blurted it out, surprising even himself. He had not realized until that moment how much Moose already meant to him.

Aunt Amanda raised an eyebrow.

Charles knew what that meant. Good luck convincing his parents that they needed another dog. Especially one the size of a small pony. Especially one who was scared of his own shadow. Charles sighed and trudged off to bed, with Moose tagging along behind him.

CHAPTER TEN

Charles woke up early the next morning, just as the sun's first rays were working their way through the window shades. "Come on, Moose," he said. "We were cooped up inside all afternoon yesterday. Let's get outside while the sun is shining." Who knew how long it would be before the next storm blew in?

He slipped into his jeans and sneakers, clipped Moose's leash on, and grabbed a banana for himself and a handful of dog biscuits for the big puppy. "I bet we'll be back before Aunt Amanda even wakes up," he whispered to Moose, but he scrawled a quick note just in case. *Off to the stream. Be back soon. — Charles and Moose.*

They set off across the meadow, Moose ambling at Charles's side. The long grass was wet with dew and Charles's sneakers were soaked through in seconds. But he didn't care. It was a beautiful morning, totally quiet except for the birdsong echoing from the trees along the edges of the field.

Charles had not forgotten his failures from the night before, but now he could not help feeling better and more hopeful as he and Moose walked along. It was hard to be in a bad mood on such a perfect morning.

They entered the woods, and soon Charles was busy watching his footing on the rocky, rooty path. He remembered being pulled along this very path on his belly just two days earlier, when Moose had freaked out over seeing a snake. "Hey," Charles said to Moose now. "I just realized something. We passed the spot where the snake was, and you didn't even pause." He reached into his pocket. "Good boy, Moose," he said, tossing a biscuit into the big dog's mouth. "Maybe you really are learning."

Moose snapped up the biscuit and swallowed it within seconds.

Yum! How about another one?

Charles laughed. "You want another, don't you?" He tossed Moose one more biscuit. Then they walked on down to the little pool by the waterfall, and Moose waded in and took a long, slurping drink.

The sky was still blue overhead, so Charles decided to follow the stream a little farther, just to see where it went. "Come on, Moose." He tugged on the leash when the big dog hesitated.

We never went that way before. Will it be scary?

"It's okay, Moose. I'll take care of you," said Charles. "Let's go." He tapped his thigh and Moose began to trot at his side as they made their way through the ferns and mossy boulders along the little stream.

Soon they came out into a little clearing. The stream trickled along one side and deep woods grew up along the other. "I don't see a trail," Charles said to Moose. "I guess we'd better go back." But just as he turned around, something stepped out of the woods. An animal—a *big* animal. What was it? A deer? A horse? Charles felt his heart pounding hard. Then it dawned on him: it was a moose! A real, live, hairy brown moose, with antlers and everything. It was huge, way bigger than Charles ever could have imagined.

The moose did not look their way as it strode toward the stream. Charles froze. If they were very quiet, and if they did not move, maybe it would not see them. If it did, what would it do, Charles wondered? Would it charge them? Charles did not know anything about mooses. Meese? Mice? He giggled nervously, realizing he didn't even know the right term for more than one moose. Then he realized he'd better make sure *his* Moose didn't freak out. "Sit," Charles whispered to Moose.

Moose sat instantly at Charles's side, looking up at him for further instruction. "Good boy. Stay," whispered Charles.

The real moose must have heard him. It swung its huge head in their direction and began to move slowly toward them, its long legs bending in the most peculiar way as it ambled along.

Moose the puppy did not freak out. He did not try to run away. He did not whine and cower behind Charles. Instead, he scooted around so that he was sitting between Charles and the approaching animal.

Don't worry. I'll protect you.

A second later, the moose seemed to lose interest. It veered off toward the woods and disappeared into the thick undergrowth.

"Oh, Moose." Charles knelt down to throw his arms around the big dog. "You were so brave." Charles hugged Moose for a long time, until his pounding heart settled down. No dog had ever done anything like that for him before. Then he and Moose ran as fast as they could, all the way up the trail, through the meadow, and back to the cabin.

"Aunt Amanda!" Charles was already talking as he burst through the back door. "You won't believe what happened. Moose is the bravest puppy ever!" He stopped short when he saw that there were three other people in the kitchen: a man, a woman, and a little girl.

Moose galloped over to the girl and began to cover her face with huge, slobbery kisses. He towered over her, but she didn't seem frightened. Instead, she threw her arms around him and buried her face in his neck. "Moosey!" she said. "I missed you."

Charles looked at his aunt. "Charles, these are Moose's owners, the Brewers," she said. "They have been missing Moose so much that they decided to drive all the way up here this morning to get him."

"But I thought—" Charles began.

Al Brewer nodded. "We weren't sure we could deal with Moose's fearfulness anymore. But when he was gone this weekend the house felt so empty. We realized how much a part of our family he really is. We talked about it, and decided we want to do whatever it takes to keep him." He gave Charles a curious look.

"What did you mean about Moose being brave?" he asked.

Charles spilled out the whole story, and Aunt Amanda chimed in with her own stories about all the training Charles had done with Moose. "He really has worked magic," she told the Brewers. "I think you'll find that Moose is already well on his way to being a happier, more confident puppy."

Mr. Brewer shook Charles's hand. "We're very grateful to you," he said.

Charles tried to answer, but there was a lump in his throat. He was happy for Moose, but sad for himself. He knew his parents would probably never have agreed to keep the big pup, but he had allowed himself to dream about it.

Mrs. Brewer smiled at Charles. "You can visit him anytime," she said, as if she had read Charles's mind. "We'll need you to help us learn how to work with him."

Then the whole family surrounded Moose, petting him and kissing him and telling him how happy they were to see him again. Charles knew just how they felt about Moose, because he felt the same way about Buddy. He would miss Moose a lot, but he knew that the big puppy was going back where he belonged, with his forever family.

He reached into his pocket for his deck of cards. Caroline looked like someone who would enjoy a good magic trick.

PUPPY TIPS

Is your dog scared of anything? My dog Django used to be afraid of thunder and of mailboxes, the big blue kind on street corners.

It can be a real challenge to own an extremely fearful dog. Charles was lucky to find some ways that worked as he began to train Moose. But that was only the beginning!

If your dog is afraid of his or her own shadow, you may want to try some of the techniques Charles used with Moose. It might also be a good idea to talk to a professional dog trainer or animal behaviorist.

It can take a lot of time and a lot of patience to help a fearful dog grow into a confident, happy pet—but it's worth it! In the end, you and your dog will love each other more than ever.

Dear Reader,

I love Great Danes. There's just something about those gentle giants! A long time ago I knew a beautiful silver and black one named Hoss (one of the dogs who goes to Aunt Amanda's doggy daycare is named after him).

When I decided to write about a Great Dane puppy, I went to visit one who belongs to a friend. I had to laugh when I pulled up in the driveway and saw Hooligan's big head looking out through the top window of the door — four and a half feet from the ground! But Hooligan was as sweet and mellow as could be. I also got to visit Hooligan's breeder, where I played with a bunch of incredibly adorable ten-week-old puppies. Doing that kind of research is just about my favorite part of my job as a writer!

Yours from the Puppy Place,
Ellen Miles

P.S. To read about another adorable puppy who needs to find a great home, try NOODLE.

How to do the
Count-'Em-Out card trick:

1) Make sure you know which card is on top of the deck. Let's say here that it is the ten of clubs.

2) Shuffle the cards in front of your audience— *carefully keeping the ten of clubs, your card, on top!* (This takes some practice. Some patter is a good idea here, to take your audience's minds off what you're doing.)

3) Deal out a number of cards into a smaller pile—you can use your own lucky number or ask an audience member for theirs. Just make sure it's not a very high or very low number. Say, as you're counting, "I want you to count out some cards, just like this: one, two, three, four . . ."

4) Put the little stack you counted out back on top of the deck, and hand it to your audience

member. Tell her to count out the *same* number of cards, the same way.

5) Guess what? Your card, the ten of clubs, is now the one on top of *her* little stack.

6) Say, "Take a look at the top card on the stack you just dealt out and memorize it. Then put it back, anywhere in the deck."

7) Now you can take all the cards and shuffle them for real, or have your audience member shuffle. It doesn't matter! You know exactly which card she looked at.

8) Take the whole deck of cards and start laying them out face up, in a line across the table. When you see the card (the ten of clubs in our example) come up, pretend not to notice it and lay down about three or four more cards. Then say, "Here comes the magic! The next card I turn over will be yours." Your audience member will think you messed up the trick, since you already laid down her card.

9) Reach into the line of cards and turn that card (the ten of clubs in our example) facedown. Ha! You turned over the card she memorized! You got her.

ABOUT THE AUTHOR

Ellen Miles loves dogs, which is why she has a great time writing the Puppy Place books. And guess what? She loves cats, too! (In fact, her very first pet was a beautiful tortoiseshell cat named Jenny.) That's why she came up with a brand-new series called Kitty Corner. Ellen lives in Vermont and loves to be outdoors every day, walking, biking, skiing, or swimming, depending on the season. She also loves to read, cook, explore her beautiful state, play with dogs, and hang out with friends and family.

Visit Ellen at www.ellenmiles.net.

THE PUPPY PLACE

WHERE EVERY PUPPY FINDS A HOME

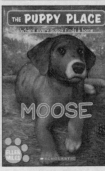